Goodnight GIANT

Once upon a time in a land filled with love, laughs, and lullabies there was a gentle Giant who had lots of little friends. The Giant played with his friends in the valley every day. But at night, when his friends returned to their cozy homes nestled in the hills, the Giant became lonely. He lay awake at night, staring into the darkness, hoping for morning when he could play with his friends again. After many sleepless nights, the Giant was REALLY tired and REALLY grumpy. When no one wanted to play with the grumpy Giant, he became even more lonely, and tired, and grumpy. Soon his sad sighs and loud grumbles kept everyone awake. The poor giant needed help falling asleep!

Calm Tom had a great idea. He remembered how his mother massaged his head with sweet lavender shampoo to help him get ready for sleep every night. So he grabbed some suds and scurried down the hill to help the Giant draw his bath.

"Ah-h-h-h," said the Giant.

Relaxed Rick knew a trick. His mom always massaged his arms and body to help him relax before bed. Rick raced to the Giant's side to give him a nice soothing rub.

The Giant smiled.

Tell Me a Story Rory could not sleep unless his dad read to him every night. Rory figured his favorite book was bound to be the answer.

The Giant liked the pictures.

Cool Jewel loved smooth talk and soft sounds to help her drift off to sleep. She decided to let the Giant listen to her most soothing songs.

The Giant hummed along.

Serene Jean needed hugs from her mom and dad AND stuffed bear whenever she snuggled into bed. Jean and her bear hurried to the valley to give their gentle friend a big hug.

Pat My Back Jack waited quietly in bed for his
grandmother to give him three tender pats at night.
Since it always helped him fall sound asleep, Jack
thought it was just what the Giant needed.

At last, the Giant closed his eyes...

And they all slept happily ever after.

Gentle Giant's Dream Routine

The Gentle Giant followed his "dream routine" each and every night helping him sleep happily every after the whole night through.

Here's a simple 3-step, before-bed routine that's been clinically proven by **JOHNSON'S®** to help toddlers fall asleep easier and sleep through the night better. Try it with your toddler!

Warm Bath

For Calm Tom and the Giant, a nighttime bath signaled the time to relax and prepare for sleep. Help your toddler relax and let go of the day's excitement with the warmth of a bath and your comforting touch. Bath time with **JOHNSON'S® BEDTIME BATH®** with NATURALCALM™ essences is part of a clinically proven routine that can help your toddler fall asleep easier and sleep through the night better. Also try **JOHNSON'S® BEDTIME WASHCLOTHS™** or **JOHNSON'S® BEDTIME MOISTURE WASH™** to enjoy the soothing aromas of NATURALCALM™ essences.

Gently Apply Lotion

Gently apply **JOHNSON'S® BEDTIME LOTION®** or **JOHNSON'S® BEDTIME TOUCH™ MASSAGE GEL** to tummy, arms, and legs, using smooth strokes. Or if you and your toddler enjoy it, try giving him a massage!

Massaging a moisturizer all over after bath time is a simple way to make your before-bed routine more relaxing for your toddler. After toweling dry, use a quarter-sized amount of gentle moisturizer to massage his arms legs, back, and tummy.

The Giant and Relaxed Rick especially liked **JOHNSON'S® BEDTIME LOTION®** and **JOHNSON'S® BEDTIME TOUCH™ MASSAGE GEL,** enriched with NATURALCALM™ essences.

Quiet Time with Mom or Dad

End your toddler's before-bed routine with quiet activities that you both enjoy, making the last activity his favorite one. Toddler age is a good age to start talking about the day. Or, enjoy singing songs or reading a favorite book together. End with hugs and kisses or, just like Pat My Back Jack, your toddler might enjoy three pats from you as the lights go out.

For more information about the JOHNSON'S® 3-step, before bed routine log on to
www.johnsonsbaby.com/sleep

Johnson's®

Quiet Time Activities

Goodnight Books

Bedtime is a quiet, calming time, and the books you choose should reflect this mood. Try not to read books that have too much exciting action or that introduce new ideas that need explaining. Books that have repetition, soothing rhythms, and themes centered on the idea of falling asleep are good choices for bedtime. Setting a limit on the number of books you read (two, for example) helps establish a consistent routine that your child can look forward to. Just like Read Me a Story Rory, he'll know what to expect and will find it comforting.

In addition to *Goodnight Giant*, you may want to include a few of these soothing tales in your bedtime library:

- *Goodnight Gorilla* by Peggy Rathman
- *Goodnight, Sleep Tight, Little Bunnies* by Dawn Apperley
- *How Do Dinosaurs Say Goodnight?* by Jane Yolen and Mark Teague
- *I'll See You in the Morning* by Mike Jolley
- *Lasso the Moon* by Trish Holland
- *Polar Bear Night* by Lauren Thompson
- *Sleep Tight, Little Mouse* by Mary Morgan
- *Song of Night: It's Time to Go to Bed* by Katie Riley Nakamura
- *Tell Me Something Happy Before I Go To Sleep* by Joyce Dunbar and Debi Gliori
- *Time for Bed* by Mem Fox and Jane Dyer

Music

Almost any kind of music that your child knows and loves can help create a restful atmosphere for sleeping. If you play a tape or CD, be sure to keep the volume low. If you are singing, slow the pace and use a lower voice to sing your little one into slumber. Don't worry about how well you sing. Your toddler will love hearing your voice no matter what! Though you may tire of singing "Twinkle, Twinkle, Little Star" over and over again, the familiarity and repetition may be just the ticket to a restful night's sleep.

Sing this bedtime song with your child and then add some of your own lyrics to the tune. For example, try replacing your child's name and the names of her favorite dolls, animals, and friends for the word "Giant" in the song.

(Sung to the tune of "Goodnight Ladies")
Good-night, Giant!
Good-night, Giant!
Good-night, Giant!
You're going to dreamland now.

Happ-i-ly you go to sleep, go to sleep, go to sleep,
Happ-i-ly you go to sleep, in your cozy bed.

Hugs

After bath, massage, books, and songs, your child will be ready for a comforting goodnight hug. A must for every bedtime routine! Your toddler may want to hug her toys and animals too just like Serene Jean did in the story. You and your child may enjoy counting hugs together as she says goodnight to you and her special toys. Ten hugs is a good limit for this part of your goodnight routine.

Pats

After lights out, your gentle touch will reassure your child and help her settle in to sleep. Try to come up with a special goodnight pat (e.g. pat her back three times, rub three times, and scratch three times before giving her a final kiss). This kind of repeated routine may work like magic to send your child to sleep.